W9-BUR-629

Serafina's Birthday

ATHENEUM   1992   NEW YORK

Maxwell Macmillan Canada
Toronto
Maxwell Macmillan International
New York   Oxford   Singapore   Sydney

Serafina's Birthday

by Alma Flor Ada

illustrated by Louise Bates Satterfield

translated from the Spanish
by Ana M. Cerro

Library of Congress Cataloging-in-Publication Data. Ada, Alma Flor. [Serafina's birthday, English] Serafina's birthday/ by Alma Flor Ada; illustrated by Louise Bates Satterfield; translated from the Spanish by Ana M. Cerro. —1st ed. p. cm. Summary: Having forgotten his present for his best friend Serafina's birthday party, Sebastian the rabbit goes to great lengths to find a replacement for it but thinks he is unsuccessful. ISBN 0-689-31516-3. [1. Rabbits—Fiction. 2. Gifts— Fiction. 3. Birthdays—Fiction. 4. Parties—Fiction.] I. Bates Satterfield, Louise, ill. II. Title. PZ7.A1857Se 1992 [E]— dc20 91-15389

For Olmo, who wanted a story
about rabbits and trains
—*A. F. A.*

With love to Paul and Calvin
—*L. B. S.*

In memory of the joyous
spirit of Samad Smith
—*A. M. C.*

Sebastian was in bed, sleeping peacefully and dreaming that he was walking through a beautiful vegetable garden. But with the sharp ring of his alarm clock, the juicy carrots and fresh, tender heads of lettuce disappeared, along with the rest of his lovely dream. Suddenly he sat straight up in bed.

"Oh, my goodness, I set the alarm wrong! It's seven forty-five!" he cried. "I'm going to miss the train, and today is Serafina's birthday!"

Sebastian jumped out of bed. He ran to his closet and pulled out some clothes. He quickly put on his pants and shirt and grabbed his jacket to put on later. Sebastian was almost out the front door when he realized that he hadn't brushed his teeth. So he retraced his steps to the bathroom.

"Who ever heard of a rabbit leaving the house without brushing his teeth?" he muttered with his mouth full of foam. He rinsed out his mouth, satisfied that he was now ready for his best friend's birthday party. But when he looked at the clock, Sebastian saw that he would have to run even faster to get to the train on time.

Sebastian arrived at the station and hopped on the train. He plopped down in his seat, pulled on his jacket, and breathed a sigh of relief. Now he could relax—he was going to arrive on time at Serafina's party after all.

"Who ever heard of a rabbit arriving late for a birthday party?" Sebastian said to himself as he settled into his seat. He was just starting to feel comfortable when it suddenly dawned on him that, in his hurry, he had forgotten to bring Serafina's birthday present.

"What can I do?" Sebastian said in despair. "Who ever heard of a rabbit going to a birthday party without bringing a present?"

Sebastian checked his pants. "Luckily, I didn't forget my wallet. I'll buy a present when I get to Rabbit Village!" Pleased that his problem was solved, he looked out the window at the rolling countryside. Gradually, the hum and the soft, rocking motion of the train made Sebastian drowsy, and he fell asleep.

"Rabbit Village! The next stop is Rabbit Village!" the conductor called out as he came down the aisle. For the second time that morning, Sebastian awoke with a start. He rubbed his eyes and hurried off the train.

"Thank goodness the conductor called out the stop," Sebastian said aloud to himself. "Who knows where I would have ended up if he hadn't. Now there is no time to waste. I must buy a present for Serafina!"

But as Sebastian walked along Main Street, he discovered that all the stores were closed. "How could I have forgotten that it is Sunday?" he said. "What am I going to do?"

Then Sebastian remembered the dream he had had that morning. "I know what I'll do," he said with a big smile. "I'll get some lettuce. Serafina adores lettuce. It's certainly

not as fancy as the embroidered handkerchief I bought for
her, but at least it's a present."

Again feeling pleased that his problem was solved,
Sebastian set off to find a vegetable garden. He soon found
one on the outskirts of Rabbit Village. The heads of lettuce
looked delicious: big, tender, and very fresh. One of these
will make a fine gift for Serafina, Sebastian thought.

But a large cat, who had been basking peacefully in the sun, did not quite agree. As Sebastian bent down to pick a head of lettuce, the cat jumped up and charged at him, making an awful hissing sound. Sebastian barely had enough time to make it over the fence and back onto the road. It was a narrow escape.

Sweaty and covered with dust, Sebastian stopped alongside a white fence to catch his breath. On the other side of the fence he saw a cabbage patch.

I'm not sure Serafina likes cabbage very much, he thought. But sometimes, when there is no lettuce, cabbage will do just as well.

Sebastian scurried underneath the white fence that
separated the cabbage patch from the road. Just as he found
a lovely leafy head of cabbage and started to pull it out of
the ground, the big shaggy dog that watched over the

cabbage patch spotted Sebastian and began to growl.
Sebastian looked up to see the dog baring his teeth at him.
For the second time that day Sebastian found himself
running for safety as fast as he could.

By the time Sebastian's train had pulled into the Rabbit Village station, guests had already begun to arrive at Serafina's birthday party. The first to arrive was Serafina's cousin Matilda, who brought a box of chocolates. Then came her neighbor Ralph, with a game of Monopoly to play. Later came Esmeralda, Frederick, Eugene, and Aurora, each bringing a present. Serafina served them all cookies and lemonade. But when Matilda asked when they were going to cut the cake, Serafina said, "We have to wait for Grandfather, who will tell us some of his wonderful stories, and for Sebastian, who promised to come, too."

Meanwhile, Sebastian was running as far as his legs could carry him. Just hearing the angry dog's barking in the distance made his ears and whiskers tremble. Finally, he sat down to rest beneath a tree. He had been sitting there for a few minutes when a nut fell by his side. Still feeling frightened, Sebastian jumped. But then he laughed.

"What luck," he said happily. "Perhaps I have found a present after all. Serafina loves to eat nuts. I'll take some of these to her." And he began to gather some nuts that had fallen to the ground.

"Just what do you think you're doing?" shouted a squirrel, descending from the top of the tree.

Sebastian looked up at the angry squirrel. "I am collecting some nuts to give to my friend as a birthday present. You see—"

"Get out of here, you thief!" shouted another squirrel from a branch. "We won't let you take those nuts. They are ours!"

"We store them for the winter. They're food for our children!" added the first squirrel.

Not wanting to anger the squirrels any further, Sebastian dropped the nuts he had gathered and left. "It's obvious that I'm not going to find a present," Sebastian muttered gloomily. "And who ever heard of a rabbit going to a birthday party without a present?"

Sebastian continued down the road to Serafina's house, kicking a small stone along the way. Soon he came to a tree laden with ripe plums. "They won't make a great gift," Sebastian thought out loud, "but they're certainly better than nothing."

So Sebastian climbed up the tree trunk and started to pick some plums. But no sooner had he picked one than a flock of birds descended on him.

"How dare you take our fruit? How dare you? How? How?" they all squawked as they circled overhead. Worrying that the birds might peck at him, Sebastian scurried down the trunk.

"I guess I'd better go to the party even though I haven't found a present. After all, who ever heard of a rabbit missing a best friend's birthday party?" Sebastian mumbled sadly to himself. And he set off, tired and unhappy, in the direction of Serafina's house.

The party had been going on for a couple of hours, but Serafina was not really having a good time. First Aunt Mireya had called saying that Grandfather was in bed with a cold, and then it seemed that Sebastian wouldn't show up either. It had been a long time since they had heard the train whistle. "What a shame that Grandfather couldn't come," said Aurora. "A birthday party without a storyteller isn't very much fun."

"What bothers me most is that Sebastian hasn't come," said Serafina. "I know that he's forgetful, but I never thought he would forget my birthday."

Then there was a knock at the door. Serafina went to answer. "He's here! Sebastian is here!" cried Serafina with delight. "I heard the train whistle a long time ago. When you didn't come, I thought you had forgotten."

"Who ever heard of a rabbit forgetting his best friend's birthday?" said Sebastian, his ears drooping sadly. "But in my hurry to catch the train I did forget something. I left your present at home," Sebastian admitted glumly.

"Oh, that doesn't matter," Serafina said with a smile. "What's important is that you are here. Come in, come in."

Sebastian was quickly surrounded by the other guests.

"Why were you so late? It's been hours since we heard the train pass," asked Matilda.

"Well, since I didn't want to come to the party without a present, and since all the stores were closed, I tried to find one," Sebastian began explaining. "And, then, one thing led to another...."

"Tell us, tell us," cried all the guests.

"Yes, please, tell us," said Serafina. "Why don't you sit here, in Grandfather's chair."

"Well, let's see," Sebastian began, taking the glass of lemonade Aurora offered him. "First I thought that I could bring some lettuce...."

And Sebastian went on to tell them how he escaped from the angry cat, from the barking dog, and from the furious squirrels who had accused him of stealing food from their children.

The rabbits listened closely, hanging on every word, and at the end of the story, when Sebastian told them how he had gotten away from the flock of angry birds, Serafina exclaimed, "And you said you didn't bring a present! Why, Sebastian, you brought the best present of all—an adventure story!"

Sebastian crossed his legs and leaned back in the chair, just as Grandfather does when he finishes a story. He took a long sip of lemonade—and smiled.